# Three Gifts
## A Christmas Trilogy

Abby Phillips

Enora Books

**Other works by the author**

I Come to the Garden Alone:
Meditations from a Psalmist's Heart

Refined by Fire:
Discovering Victory through Adversity
*(featured author)*

A Drink from the Well:
Refreshment for the Soul *(featured author)*

This is a work of fiction. Any similarities between the fictional characters in this book and any person, living or deceased, is purely coincidental.

Three Gifts: A Christmas Trilogy

ISBN-13: 9780984717408
Cover image © Okea | Dreamstime.com

# Robby and Tammy's Gift

But now faith, hope, love, abide these three;
but the greatest of these is love.
– 1 Corinthians 13:13

*November 26*

"All I said was that I hope the art galleries like my work. You know selling my art is how I make my money, Robby. Why are you being so touchy?"

"Whatever. You're just whining because you didn't want to make this move. Now you're going to make me miserable about it every step of the way."

"Oh good grief! I can't believe this! Everything has to be about you! *You* can complain that the airline doesn't carry your precious bagged walnuts. *You* can go on and on about how you hope there are good barber shops to keep your hair looking perfect. But if *I* voice a concern suddenly it's a conspiracy! Believe me, if I felt that passionately about not leaving Chicago, I would have just stayed there and you could have left by yourself."

The flight attendant discreetly approached the arguing couple. "Sir? Ma'am? I'm sorry, but I'm going to have to ask you to lower your voices so you won't disturb the other passengers."

Robby and Tammy Franklin gladly complied and spent the remainder of the flight in one of the greatest cold shoulder battles ever seen on Earth.

For a young couple beginning a new life in a different state, this was not a very good start.

The Franklins had been married two years, four months, and twenty-two days. Somewhere in year one, around month ten, they had secretly begun wondering how long it would be until the marriage was over.

As things had grown worse, they thought a fresh start in a new place might help them slow down from the hustle and bustle of big city life enough to save their marriage. Robby put in for a transfer at the bank, they sold their condo, and right after Thanksgiving they headed to their new home in Fredericksburg, Virginia.

It wasn't a good sign that they couldn't even manage to remain civil for the four-hour plane trip.

The stony silence continued the full length of the car ride. When they finally pulled up in front of their lovely new Cape Cod style home with its attached garage, they unpacked quickly and with few words, completely ignoring the inviting façade and picturesque neighborhood as effectively as they were ignoring each other.

*December 1*

"Hi, Mom!" Tammy was glad she'd stopped working on her latest painting to answer her cell phone. She was feeling a little homesick and a call from her mother was just what she needed.

"Well, it's been a week now, and I sure do miss you, sweetie. How's it been going so far?"

"I miss you and Dad too. The weather's gorgeous. I can't believe how warm it is. Christmas is only a few weeks away and it still feels like October!"

She saw a spot she'd missed on the canvas and dabbed at it gently with her brush. "Even though I don't miss the bone-chilling cold, I don't know how I feel about not having a white Christmas."

"Really? I was positive that it snowed there."

"I guess it does, but not as much as we get back home and it looks like this year we actually might not get any at all. There's definitely none on the ground right now."

"Well, hopefully you'll get your snow-covered lawn in time for Christmas. Hold on, your father's saying something … What, dear? Oh! … He says that if you don't, he'll ship you some of ours."

Tammy laughed. "Tell Dad I just might take him up on that."

"So are you both settled in yet?"

"Yeah. Apparently we're settled in enough for Robby to go back to his 12-hour workdays at the bank. So much for a fresh start."

"Oh sweetie, I'd hoped this move would really help you both reconnect. What's happening?"

Tammy set her paintbrush down, collapsed in a nearby easy chair, and massaged her forehead, heedless of the paint splatters she dusted on her face in the process.

"I wish I knew," she sighed. "When I first met him, we personified that 'opposites attract' saying. It had nothing to do with the whole Black-White couple thing. He was quiet where I was loud; I was unpredictable where he was consistent. We balanced each other out. I helped him use more of his right brain, and he taught me to focus my energy."

Little did she know that not too far away a similar conversation was taking place.

"Now it seems like the things that drew us to each other are driving us crazy," Robby explained to his father during his lunch break. "She's like this hippie flower child; an irresponsible person with no long-term goals in her life."

"He's so predictable and systematic, like a robot," Tammy continued. "There's no passion, no vision for what he wants for the rest of his life."

"Dad, I just wish I could get back what I used to have with her."

"Mom, I just wish I could get back what I used to have with him."

At the end of those identically desperate and hurting conversations, another set of similar conversations began to take place.

"Father, fix what's broken between those two," Robby's parents prayed. "We saw the love they had for each other on their wedding day. Show them how to get that back. Remind them of what's really important."

"Lord, restore the love they once had," Tammy's mother and father prayed. "Let them remember why they fell in love in the first place."

The Franklins would soon come to thank God for praying parents.

## ❧ 3 ❦

*December 3*

"Whatcha got?" Tammy asked as Robby stepped in the front door reading a postcard. He'd just returned from his Saturday morning jog.

"'Ripe Harvest Fellowship welcomes you to our neighborhood'," he read aloud. "We'd love for you to join us for worship this Sunday." He arched an eyebrow as he glanced at her. "Somebody's hospitality ministry is really on its job."

Tammy's heart fluttered. How long had it been since he'd made that playful face and used that joking tone?

"Wanna go?" she asked nonchalantly, afraid to disrupt the peaceful moment.

"You know, maybe we should," he replied, kicking off his scruffy running shoes. "We haven't been to church in a while. I'm game if you are."

Considering the state of affairs in the Franklin house, comparing the conversation to successful peace talks between nations wasn't too much of a stretch.

The next morning, after a couple of false starts ("I wonder if I have to wear a skirt", "Do you think I should put on a tie?") they made the short drive to Ripe Harvest Fellowship.

They'd decided to dress conservatively for their first visit and discovered, to their great delight, that they were overdressed. They were also happy to see the many ethnicities represented there. There were some places, including churches, where even in this day and age their mixed marriage caused quite the stir.

As the praise and worship segment of the service began Tammy's gaze was drawn to Robby as he sang along to the lively praise song. She felt her heartbeat quicken as she watched him with his caramel skin, close-cut immaculate haircut, and lean build. Listening to his strong tenor voice reminded her of when they met in the community choir back in Chicago.

"God, our love was strong once. Please make it that way again," she prayed quietly. It felt good to pray. Somewhere in the middle of the chaos of their marriage, their church attendance had dropped off and eventually their prayer lives had ceased too. Being here reminded her of the comfort of God's love and His abiding presence. The habit of praying came back so quickly that it was as if it never left.

The song ended and the band moved seamlessly into another. This one was Tammy's favorite and she sang with her eyes closed and her heart more open than it had been in months.

Now it was Robby's turn to watch his wife with a quickening pulse. Her fiery red hair was vibrant against her pale, freckled skin as she stretched out her hands in worship. She still had that lilting soprano voice he'd found so lovely when he first met her in that community choir back home.

"Lord, give us back what we've lost," he prayed. "I don't even know how we lost it. I just know I want it back."

On the drive home, Tammy mentioned that she enjoyed the service.

"Yeah, I did too," Robby agreed. "I'd like to go back next week."

"Me too!"

"I saw in the bulletin that they have groups for couples, singles, and youth throughout the week. What do you think about checking out a Tuesday evening couples' group?"

Tammy was stunned. "But ... you never want to do anything on weeknights. You're always at work."

Robby's defenses shot up. "You know what? Never mind."

"Come on, Robby. You can't just drop a shocker like that on me and expect me not to be surprised. You're never home!"

"You know what I can't figure out? How a normal conversation about making plans to attend a church service turned into an argument about my work habits! Forget I even mentioned it."

Robby pulled into the attached garage and jumped out of the car. Without another word he stormed into the house and locked himself in the office. Checking his e-mails and surfing the Internet would help take his mind off his sham of a relationship with his wife.

Tammy sat numbly in the car. "So much for thinking going to church would make a difference," she whispered. After several more minutes she quietly entered the house and closeted herself in the bedroom. Maybe a long nap buried beneath the covers would take her mind off the mess her marriage had become.

## ❧ 4 ❧

*December 6*

"So, you're a painter," the elderly African-American woman commented.

Tammy was in a quaint arts and crafts shop she'd discovered. She was stocking up on drop cloths and oil paint, but she couldn't find the brush set she was looking for.

"Yes, I am. Do you paint?"

"No, child. I like to make little gifts for people. I used to knit, but old Uncle Arthur got a hold of my fingers and now I can't do that anymore. I've been trying my hand at making gift baskets lately, and I'm here to pick up a few things."

"It's been a long time since anyone's called me 'child'," Tammy responded with a faint smile.

"Oh, I hope I didn't offend you."

"No, it's not that at all. My grandmother used to call me that. She's gone now, and it just reminded me of how much I miss her."

"I understand. We old folks do tend to call you younger ones 'child' don't we? I guess when you're as ancient as I am, everybody under the age of forty is a child," she laughed as she spoke. "I'd love to see some of your paintings sometime," she added.

"I'd love to see some of your gift baskets too. I enjoy giving personalized gifts to family and friends. Maybe I can buy some baskets from you." Tammy handed the woman her business card.

She perched her bifocals on the tip of her nose and read aloud. "Tammy Franklin. Well, Tammy Franklin, I'm Ella Winslow, and it's a pleasure to meet you."

"It's very nice to meet you, too. Please do call me. It would be wonderful to talk about our crafts."

"I certainly will." Ella Winslow placed the business card in her purse with the slow care of someone who has learned with time that there are very few things worth rushing over. "You have a blessed day, child." She winked at Tammy and continued down the aisle.

The pleasant encounter stayed with Tammy the rest of the day, as did the blessing Ella bestowed on her. It reminded her of church, which made her think about the couples' group that was meeting that night. As she was putting her art supplies away, she pondered in frustration that she had really wanted to attend. If only Robby hadn't been so stubborn.

Since they had no children yet, Tammy had converted one of the three bedrooms into her art studio. She could have set up shop in the office, but that would have been much more trouble than it was worth because of Robby. He didn't mind her painting. As a matter of fact, he admired her work. He just didn't want anything to do with the actual process.

He didn't like the smell of her oil paints; he was terrified that she was going to spill them on a hardwood floor or some leather upholstery; and he absolutely balked at the cost of replenishing brushes and paint tubes. For the sake of peace she kept everything having to do with her craft out of his way until the project was done.

Once she got paid for her work though, he always became an avid art lover. That thought irritated her even more and before long, she'd worked herself into quite a mood.

When he called to say he had to work late again that evening, it was the last straw. She decided that, husband or not, she was going to the couples' group. Maybe she'd learn something that would help her with her impossible man.

Robby really didn't have to catch up on anything at work that night. He just wanted a little peace and quiet, which seemed impossible to find at home. As the hour hand on the clock moved closer to seven, his mind wandered to the couples' group at church. He had really wanted to go. If only Tammy hadn't gotten so combative when he'd brought it up.

Maybe attending the group by himself would give him some answers or support. If something didn't happen soon, he was about ready to call the whole thing off.

## ❧ 5 ❧

"Father, we thank You for this time we have together. May it glorify You and edify Your people. Help us, dear Lord, as we seek to reflect Your love and unity in our marriages. We ask it in Jesus' name. Amen."

Minister Jerry Flakes closed the couples' group prayer, looked up, and began smiling so profusely that everyone, including Tammy, instinctively followed his gaze.

"Well, praise God! Tammy didn't think you'd be able to make it. We're so glad you did!"

Every face in the small circle displayed the same happiness to see him. Every face but one.

Robby noticed that Tammy's cheeks blushed bright red, and her expression of surprise and embarrassment mirrored his own. As he took the empty seat next to his wife, they both struggled to regain their composure. Thankfully, few people noticed the awkward moment, and those who did tactfully declined to comment on it.

"Tonight we're going to look at two stories, both involving King David," Minister Jerry began. "The first one is found in 1 Samuel 25."

After reading the passage, he closed his Bible. "So Nabal was a rich, powerful businessman who was also corrupt. David sent some of his men to speak peacefully with Nabal, but he insulted the king. David was ready to attack him, but his wife, Abigail, who was as wise as she was beautiful, went to King David carrying gifts and pled for mercy."

"If it hadn't been for her, Nabal and his men would have been killed. The next day, when she told her husband what happened, his heart failed and ten days later he died. When David found out he was dead, he married Abigail."

"What a big knothead Nabal was," one woman muttered, and chuckles filled the room.

"No kidding," another woman responded. "I mean, this was a big guy who liked to throw his weight around and belittle his wife. Then she had to try and calm King David down after Nabal put his foot in his mouth."

"Right away we see something we can learn," Minister Jerry added. "We should each examine ourselves to see if we're walking in humility, or if we're imposing our wills on our spouses. Are we constantly rubbing people the wrong way? Are our husbands or wives on regular cleanup patrol, trying to apologize for hurtful things we've said or done to others? It's not my wife's job to clean up my mess."

"Thank you, darlin'," Karen Flakes replied gently and patted him on the hand. More good-natured laughter filled the room.

Minister Jerry flashed a quick, doting smile to his wife, and continued. "If I don't like having to clean it up either, then I shouldn't make it. So to avoid that problem, we should do what?"

"Be mindful of how we speak to and treat people in general and our spouses in particular," a young woman answered.

"Exactly. As married couples, we're here to love each other and build one another up. Nobody is anybody else's doormat. As a result of his heart and attitude towards the man of God, Nabal died. Because of her wisdom and gentle spirit, Abigail became King David's wife."

"The second passage we're going to look at is 2 Samuel 6. I know most of you are familiar with this one. Karen, will you read it?"

The group listened intently as the minister's wife read the chapter. Once she finished, he continued. "The ark was finally returned to Jerusalem and David was rejoicing and dancing before the Lord. His wife, Michal, saw him from a window and got angry. He began blessing the people, but when he came to bless his own household, Michal met him at the door and pretty much let him have it for dancing in the street and making a fool of himself."

"David told her that he was willing to be undignified in worship before God who had raised him up as king. After that, Michal became barren."

One large, burly man spoke up. "What a sorry welcome home. As men, respect is really important. I just cringe when I think about how excited King David was about God's blessing, and how his wife's disrespect must have hurt him."

"Yeah! Didn't she understand the spiritual significance of the return of the ark?" another man chimed in. "I hear women say all the time that they wish guys would be more demonstrative in worship. Yet here's a man who's worshipping unashamed before the Lord, and his wife just verbally flays him."

Minister Jerry shook his head enthusiastically at the lively conversation. "You both mentioned something key. Ralph, you brought up respect. Dave, you touched on understanding where the other person is coming from - why they do what they do. That's good stuff!"

Karen chuckled. "Honey, did you notice that when we read about Nabal acting up, the women had comments, but when Michal was in the wrong, the men spoke up?"

After a moment of silent realization everyone began to laugh.

"Many times the problems we're talkin' about play themselves out just like we're seein' here. The most common complaints that we hear are that wives feel their husbands don't listen to them or value them; and husbands feel their wives don't respect them."

"Yet the word of God provides a clear solution for these kinds of relationship breakdowns," she continued. "Ephesians 5:25 tells husbands to love their wives as Christ loved the church and gave His life for her. It goes on to say that wives are to honor and respect their husbands. Do you know how many marriages would be healthier if couples just followed those instructions?"

Hearty amens were heard all around the room. The Franklins sat in silent conviction as they held their behavior toward one another up to God's standard and realized just how far off the mark they'd gotten.

Minister Jerry stood. "Well everyone, we had a great conversation tonight. Our time's up. Feel free to stick around for some snacks after prayer. Ralph, would you close us out?"

The husky man who had spoken earlier bowed his head. "Lord, thank You for the time we've had tonight. You showed us in Your Word what we should and shouldn't do in our marriages. Help us to be doers of the Word and not hearers only. In Christ's name, Amen."

There was a chorus of amens, and then the group made a beeline for the refreshment table to enjoy the spread. There were carafes of coffee and hot water for tea and hot chocolate next to a stack of Styrofoam cups and stir sticks. A couple of serving platters were filled with snickerdoodles, doughnut holes, and oatmeal raisin cookies.

Minister Jerry patted Robby on the back and handed him a steaming cup of coffee. "I'm really glad the both of you could make it tonight. I hope you enjoyed yourselves."

Robby cleared his throat. "We definitely needed this. You guys put a pretty big spotlight on some stuff we need to fix. I'm glad we came."

"Yeah," Tammy agreed softly as she approached the table to make some hot chocolate.

"We all struggle in our marriages sometimes," the middle-aged man replied comfortingly.

"Don't let anybody tell ya otherwise," Karen added as she sailed by with a handful of cookies.

With a laugh, the minister continued. "As long as we show agape love to our spouses, we'll see them as God's children, we'll want what God wants for them, and we'll treat them with honor and respect. That kind of love will help us overcome a whole lot of problems."

The couple sat quietly in the living room. Both wanted to say something, but neither knew exactly how to say it. Finally Tammy worked up the nerve to speak.

"I was really surprised to see you there tonight. I thought you didn't want to go."

Robby sighed. "I never said I didn't want to go. I planned on getting off of work on time so we *could* go." He rubbed his face tiredly with his hands. "But then you lit into me about working late, and I thought *you* didn't want to go. I just didn't feel like arguing, especially after the great time we had at service, so I just dropped it."

Tammy abandoned the easy chair and joined Robby on the couch. "I'm sorry I snapped at you like that. For so long now, I've felt like you'd rather spend time with anyone in the world but me. The defensiveness and hurt I felt in my heart came out of my mouth. I apologize, Robby. Please forgive me."

He searched her face and was touched by the sincerity he saw there. It pricked his conscience and he sighed with regret. "If I had paid more attention to how you felt about me working late, you wouldn't have had all that bottled up inside of you in the first place. I'm asking you to forgive me too."

Tammy leaned in to hug him. He accepted the embrace and encircled her in his arms.

He breathed deeply, finding comfort in closeness they hadn't experienced for far too long.

It affected her too. She tried to fight them, but tears began to stream down her face, and she started to sob softly.

"What is it, baby?" he whispered as he rubbed her back gently.

"It's just been so long since we've really talked to one another or held each other. It's been months since we've been intimate. I miss what we had so much." Her voice shook with emotion as she fought to speak. "I miss you."

He wiped her tears away with the pads of his thumbs. "I miss you too."

"I don't want to miss you anymore, Robby."

He searched her eyes and found the same loneliness and longing he felt.

"Then let's start fresh. Tonight. Right now. I wanna live everyday in agape love with you. Are you game?"

She sniffed and smiled. "I'm game."

The kiss they shared was as gentle and sweet and full of promise as everything that came after it.

*December 17*

"Hello there, Tammy. It's Ella."

Tammy's face lit up as she held the phone. "Hi, there! I'm so glad you called. How are you?"

"Oh, very well, and yourself?"

"Much better than I've been in a while!"

"Well praise the Lord," Ella exclaimed. "I'm glad to hear it. I called to see how your painting was coming, but I'm always ready to join a good testimony service!"

Tammy laughed. "Oh, I can definitely testify! My husband, Robby, and I have found a church home, we've been going to a wonderful couples group, and we're even getting marriage counseling from the pastor." She hesitated. "I can't believe I'm telling you all of this. We hardly know each other!"

"True enough, but we're sisters in Christ, and sometimes you can just feel that bond. I'm so glad things are getting better between you and your husband. Marriage is hard work, but it's worth it."

"My Eddie's been gone for two years," she continued. "We used to wear on each other's nerves from time to time, but we loved each other. Not a day goes by that I don't think about him or miss him. Treasure that man of yours. Tomorrow's not promised to any of us, so we've got to appreciate our blessings every day we're alive."

Tammy felt tears begin to form as the elderly woman spoke. "I sure will, Ella. Thank you."

"You're more than welcome." The older woman's voice lit up. "By the way, I'm working on several gift baskets to take to some of my friends at the nursing home. They don't get company as often as they'd like, so some friends of mine and I have started visiting them, talking about old times and the goodness of the Lord. Without Eddie, it gets mighty lonely sometimes, so those visits do me just as much good as they do my friends."

"That's so awesome, Ella." Tammy was touched by her new friend's giving spirit. "Hey, would you be willing to make a small gift basket for my husband? Nothing elaborate. Just a small 'I love you' gift."

Ella chuckled. "Things must be going really well if you're thinking about 'just because' gifts. I believe I've got just the thing."

The two women plotted companionably for a few more minutes before hanging up, and then Tammy immediately placed another phone call.

"Hi, Mom. Listen, a lot has changed since we last talked. I have so much to tell you!"

Once again, not too far away, a similar conversation was taking place.

"Son, I'm so glad to hear that things are better for you two." Robby's father rejoiced when he got the news that his son and daughter-in-law's marriage was on the mend. "Nobody can tell me that our God won't answer prayer!"

"You better talk about it! God is able!" That was Robby's mother yelling out in the background. He smiled at the joy he heard in her voice.

"I want to thank you two for praying for us, man. It means a lot to me – to both of us."

"We pray for you because you mean a lot to *us*. We love you, Robert."

"I love you and Mom too, Dad."

Robby put his cell phone away as he walked into the hardware store.

"Mornin', Mr. Franklin," the store clerk called. Robby and Tammy had been making so many little updates to the house that the store staff knew them by name.

"Morning, Fernando," Robby called back. "Hey, you got a minute? I need your advice on something."

"Sure thing. What can I do for you?"

Pointing to a shelf of bags, he asked "Which one of these is better?"

It took Fernando a moment to recover from the shock. This customer was something of a miser when it came to money. He always looked for sale items and he always bought the cheapest version of whatever he was looking for. Now he was asking about the quality of a product rather than its cost.

"Well, this one costs the least, but the stuff looks like shredded plastic. This one's more expensive, but it looks like the real deal. If you're looking for good quality, sometimes you gotta pay extra for it."

"Understood. Thanks for the help."

"No problem." Fernando walked back to his register, and then watched in amazement as Robby began to fill up his entire shopping cart with the good stuff.

## ❧ 8 ❦

*Christmas Eve*

Christmas Eve service at Ripe Harvest Fellowship was truly something to write home about.

There were decorative poinsettias artfully placed all around the sanctuary and foyer. The children did an adorable skit reenacting the nativity, complete with costumes and props. The choir did a variety of Christmas songs, from the classic Hallelujah Chorus to modern Christmas songs by contemporary Christian artists. The praise dancers performed in their beautiful shimmering gowns, twirling ribbons as they leapt down the aisles.

The spirit of joy was tangible and contagious. Robby and Tammy couldn't stop smiling at one another. Things had gotten so much better since they'd reconnected with God and a loving church. Of course they still had their problems, but the couples' group and counseling were really helping, and they were learning day by day to be more loving and respectful of one another, even when they didn't agree.

They had taken Minister Jerry's words to heart: "Remember to listen more than you speak. That's why God gave us two ears and one mouth."

Pastor Hargate's message was "Love Came Down." As he shared the Christmas story, he reminded the congregation that love was God's motivation for everything that Christ did. He closed by exhorting everyone to allow love to be the motivation for their thoughts, words, and actions as well.

Afterwards there was a festive gathering in the fellowship hall with punch, hot apple cider, cake, and lots of laughter.

On the car ride home, Tammy sighed. "That was such an awesome service. I'm so thankful for all the newness God has given us."

"I sense a 'but' coming," Robby replied sagely.

Tammy laughed. "Yeah, you do. I'll get over it, but I just wish we could've gotten a little snow on Christmas Day."

"We may yet. You never know," Robby said with a secret smile. "My dad always says 'Don't tell me God won't answer prayer.'"

The next morning Tammy awoke to find her husband's side of the bed empty. She burrowed her feet into her slippers and went downstairs to find him. She soon located him standing in the kitchen sipping a cup of hot chocolate.

He looked up when she walked in the room, smiled, and handed her a steaming mug. "Merry Christmas, you."

"Merry Christmas, you", she whispered as she accepted the mug and the kiss that came with it.

"Before we open presents, I want to give you a 'just because' gift. I know how much you love to look and smell good. Well, I love how good you look and smell too, so I asked a friend to put this together." She pulled out Ella's handiwork and handed it to him.

"Wow." He let out a low whistle as he held the gift basket up for inspection. In it were a set of Andes beard and mustache trimmers, and a small travel set of his favorite cologne and aftershave lotion, nestled in a bed of his beloved walnut halves.

He hugged her and kissed her forehead. "Thank you! This is fantastic!"

"You're welcome." She helped him pull the pretty gold cellophane off the basket, and then popped a piece of walnut in his mouth.

"Mm. Girl, you know I love me some walnuts. Now," he said dramatically. "I've got a 'just because' surprise for you too."

She clapped her hands and squealed with so much childlike excitement that he had to give her a quick kiss on the nose. "Come outside with me."

She accepted his outstretched hand and followed him to the front door.

"I know how much you really wanted a white Christmas this year."

"Oooh, Robby! Did it snow last night?"

"No, but I hope this is a pretty decent substitute. Fernando at the hardware store said it looks like the real deal." With a flourish, he opened the door and beckoned for her to go outside.

There was a sharp intake of breath. Two hands flew to an open mouth. Tears began to flow down a face full of wonder.

The entire front lawn was covered with artificial snow. Everything from the grass to the mums and hostas to the trimmed evergreen shrubs sported a coat of white powder.

"Do you like it?" he whispered behind her.

"Yes. Yes!" She launched herself into his arms, and he laughed and lifted her off the ground. "Mom was right! I got my snow-covered lawn after all. I know it must have cost you a fortune, but I love it!"

He set her down and rubbed his nose against hers. "It definitely wasn't cheap and it's gonna be a bear to clean up, but I wanted to make your Christmas wish come true."

"Oh, Robby. You did. We got a second chance to make our marriage work, and now this. God's been good to me. I couldn't ask for more."

He would love his new running shoes, and she would be ecstatic over her sable paintbrush set, but the best gifts that year – renewed love and a snow angel contest on the only snow-covered lawn in the neighborhood – were the most precious things Robby and Tammy Franklin would remember from that very special Christmas.

# Fernando's Gift

"For I know the plans that I have for you,"
declares the LORD, "plans for welfare
and not for calamity to give you
a future and a hope."
- Jeremiah 29:11

*November 26*

Fernando Rodriguez ran his hands through his thinning black hair and wondered for the twentieth time if he should try that Rogaine stuff or just shave it all off. Lots of men sported bald heads these days, so you really couldn't tell who was doing it as a fashion statement and who was doing it because the doughnut hole in his dome kept getting bigger.

He took his time balancing the cash register drawer and shutting off the lights. He had nowhere to go but home, and there wasn't anybody to go home to.

Holidays could be hard for a single guy. Most of his friends and relatives that were his age were married, and the ones who weren't didn't want to be. He was thankful for his large family – he never had to spend a holiday alone. But once the festivities were over, he always had to go back to an empty house.

He set the alarm, and as it began to beep he made a beeline out of the hardware store and locked the door and security gate behind him. No matter how well he performed that routine, knowing the alarm would start roaring if he didn't get out in fifty seconds always sent him running.

He stopped off at old Mrs. Winslow's house to deliver the Christmas lights she'd given him money to buy for her. She lived a few doors down from him and had lost her husband a couple of years before. He checked on her from time to time to see if she needed her lawn mowed or something repaired. In return she'd often share a cup of coffee and some pleasant conversation with him. One time she even gave him a hand-knitted scarf. He prayed for her loneliness nearly every time he prayed for his own.

Once he got home, he changed into a tee shirt and sweats, and spent some time looking for youth ministry tools on the Internet. He loved working with the little kids at church, and he was always trying to find different ways to engage them.

He found a couple of good sites and made some notes until his eyes started to sting. He finally powered down his computer at one o'clock in the morning and stumbled off to bed.

## ☙ 2 ❧

*November 27*

"Mr. Rodriguez!" The class of five- through eight-year-olds at Blessed Savior Church screamed as their teacher came in the door.

Fernando often joked that the reason he loved working with the kids was that they made him feel like a rock star whenever he walked into a room.

"Hey there, alumnos!" he yelled back.

"Are you gonna tell us a story today?" a little girl named Sarah asked.

Fernando was gifted at spinning stories that captivated the kids and he always seemed to effortlessly weave Christian values into every little tale he told. Some of the other workers would even come by his room sometimes to listen.

"I sure am," he replied and shouts of excitement filled the room.

For the next several minutes he mesmerized them with a story about a brother and sister and a magical wish-granting dragon.

The students sat cross-legged on the floor, listening intently as he explained how the children in the story became more and more selfish with their wishes until finally they had an awful fight. It was only then that they remembered God wants His people to care about helping others more than they care about getting stuff for themselves.

"So what happened to the dragon when they stopped being selfish?" one of the boys asked.

"Poof!" Fernando made the sound with his mouth and gestured with his hands as if the dragon disintegrated into the air. "He couldn't tempt them to be selfish and to fight anymore. He lost his power, so he disappeared."

The kids all clapped and cheered.

"The dragon was the devil, right Mr. Rodriguez?" the same boy asked.

"Yes, Hector. He sure was. Very good!"

"He tries to make us be selfish and fight just like the kids in the story. But if we remember to love like God loves, we can make him go away like they did!" a little girl piped in.

"That's absolutely right, Maggie. He does try to get us to be unloving toward each other, but with God's power, you can defeat Satan," Fernando beamed, proud that they'd gotten the underlying message of his story.

A little boy named Stephen jumped up and struck a superhero pose. "We can be superheroes for God!"

All the kids laughed and cheered as Fernando picked Stephen up and flew him around the room.

After the parents came to pick their little ones up, Janet, one of the other youth workers, approached

Fernando. "You have such a wonderful gift. You really should publish your stories. I mean it!" she exclaimed as she saw the look of doubt on his face. "Everyone can't just think up cool stories like that. They're so captivating and they have biblical truths kids can understand and apply. God gave you a gift. Just think about it."

"Yeah, um, okay. So how's Jeff?"

Janet rolled her dark brown eyes at the mention of the boyfriend she'd been hoping desperately would become her fiancé. "Please. I don't think I'll ever get a ring."

She began to twirl a strand of hair from her ponytail around her finger.

He knew that was a sure sign she was getting irritated.

"The proverb says that he who finds a wife finds a good thing. He doesn't realize what a good thing he's got. Maybe he'll realize it once I tell him to hit the road."

By now she was pretty worked up. All five feet three inches of her fumed with indignation.

He thought it was adorable.

"Hey!" She narrowed her eyes and lightly punched his shoulder. "Oh, no you don't. Don't you dare try to change the subject. Remember, I teach a classroom full of eight- to ten-year-old kids. I don't get distracted that easily."

Fernando playfully rubbed his offended shoulder. "Ow! Hey, a guy can try, can't he? Come on, Janet. I doubt I could ever do anything that cool. Even if I could, who would illustrate it? I mean, the drawings I try to do for my stories end up looking like a little kid made them."

"Well, if you're illustrating a children's book that can be a good thing. It would be a book for kids that looks like the pictures were drawn *by* kids. That's pretty cute when you think about it. And as much of a techie as you are, you'll never convince me that you don't have a scanner and PhotoShop in your house right now. If anything needed editing or sprucing up, you could do that too."

"You make it sound so possible, like it could really happen," he mused.

"With God, all things are possible," she replied as she patted him on the same shoulder she'd just punched him on and left the room.

≈ **3** ≈

*November 30*

Wednesday night was family night at the Rodriguez house. Fernando and all of his aunts, uncles and cousins would gather at his parents' house for potluck and card games.

Fernando stood in the kitchen with Inez Rodriguez. His mother was spry and attractive for her sixty-five years and she never let anyone forget it. She had a good and kind heart and he loved her dearly.

He watched her direct the family with the efficiency of a general. Salad was being tossed, plates and glasses were being set on the table, and desserts came out of the oven, all under her watchful eye.

"You're amazing," Fernando complimented her and kissed her cheek.

She chuckled and patted his hand. "Such a good boy. I taught you well, didn't I?"

"You didn't raise this fine young man on your own, woman. Quit hogging all the credit!"

"Hola, Papi." Fernando smiled as his father sauntered into the room and hugged him.

Ramón Rodriguez gave his wife an affectionate pat on the backside, causing her to giggle like an infatuated schoolgirl.

Fernando loved the relationship his parents had, even as his heart ached for that himself. He couldn't dwell on it too long or he'd be a real drag all evening. Instead he ate until he was full and laughed until he was sore. Still, the closer it got to the end of the evening, the more he began to feel the familiar dread of going home alone.

After nearly everyone had left, he stayed to help his mother wash dishes and clean up in the kitchen while his father tidied up the living room.

Ramón refused to let anyone else do it. That room, with its comfortable leather recliner and big screen TV, was his sanctuary, and he wanted it put back just the way he liked it.

Inez stopped drying dishes, sighed, and leaned against the kitchen counter. Fernando stopped wiping down countertops and braced himself, knowing what was coming next.

"Nando, when are you gonna finally settle down with one of these women I keep finding for you and give me beautiful nietos y nietas?"

"Ay, Mamí! I've been trying to like the ladies you set me up with but you're making it really hard for me. The one from your church has three cats, and you know I'm allergic. The one down the street from here thought she could get discounts at the hardware store because she knew me. And the last one," he finished with a shiver. "Her mustache is almost as big as abuelo's. That's just wrong!"

"Stop it!" She laughed as she smacked his arm. "Her mustache isn't that bad. Besides, if my matchmaking skills are so awful, why aren't you looking for someone yourself?" she pouted.

"I'm going to bed now, Inez. I'm an old man and I'm tired. Buenas noches, Nando."

"Buenas noches," Fernando and his mother called, stifling their laughter at the older man's blunt statement. Since they were finished with the kitchen, they went to sit in the living room.

Fernando collapsed on the couch and sighed heavily. "I *am* looking myself, but who wants to date a thirty-five-year-old, balding hardware store clerk? You may think I'm great, and I appreciate that. But to most women, I'm nobody. I can't say I blame them for feeling that way. I don't even know what I'm supposed to be doing with my life."

Inez knelt in front of him and grasped his face in her hands. "Fernando Miguel Rodriguez, you listen to me! You are my son and I'm proud of you. You are a child of God and He loves you. No matter what your life looks like, you always remember that. Understand? God has a purpose for your life, and it will come to pass in His time if you'll pay attention to what He tells you."

"And if He has someone for you, He'll send her your way when He's ready and not a second before. Until then, I'll keep my mouth shut about you giving me grandchildren and I'll even close down my pitiful matchmaking business. Okay?"

Fernando had to laugh as he hugged his mother and accepted her kiss on his forehead.

"Sí, mí corazón."

## ❧ 4 ❧

Fernando arrived home late that night and went straight to bed, so it wasn't until the next morning that he noticed the flashing red light indicating there was a message on his cell phone.

He played the voicemail and heard a familiar, troubled voice.

"Hey, it's Janet. I just wanted to let you know that Maggie, one of the little girls in your Sunday school class, was admitted to the hospital today. I was finishing my shift in the pediatric ward when they brought her in. Poor thing. I'm not sure what's wrong with her. They were still doing tests when I left. Just keep her in your prayers."

His shift didn't start until noon, so Fernando drove straight to the hospital, praying the whole way. He stopped long enough to get Maggie's room number at the registration desk, and then jogged through a maze of hallways and a small skywalk until he got to her door.

As he stepped inside, his breath caught in his throat. Maggie's seven-year-old frame looked so tiny in the hospital bed that he had to blink several times to keep from crying.

"Hi, Mr. Rodriguez," she croaked. She looked up at him with huge chocolate eyes that melted his heart.

He patted her head and smiled at her lopsided braided pigtails. "Hey there, Maggie," He lowered his voice to a whisper when he noticed her mother asleep on a cot in the corner.

"Mama says I got dye beads."

His eyebrows furrowed as he tried to grasp what she was saying.

Maggie's mom stirred behind him. She opened her eyes and for a brief moment, he could tell she'd forgotten where she was. She got her bearings almost instantly and rose from the cot, trying to stretch and yawn as politely as possible.

"I'm sorry, Mrs. Walker. I was trying not to wake you up."

"It's alright, Fernando. Thank you so much for coming to visit Maggie."

"Um, she told me that she has 'dye beads'." He shrugged his shoulders cluelessly.

Mrs. Walker smiled sadly. "Juvenile diabetes."

He felt like the bottom fell out of his stomach. He knew enough about diabetes to understand that it often meant a lifetime of shots and medication. It could be controlled, but there was no cure.

Mrs. Walker saw the shock and sadness in his face. "I know. But God was with us. When they tested her, her blood sugar was nearly 400. If we hadn't brought her in when we did..." It was clear that she was shaken to the core thinking of what could have been, and her voice was filled with emotion as she fought back tears. "I'm so thankful that God kept her safe and allowed us to get her here in time. He didn't leave us then, and He won't leave us now."

Maggie posed like a superhero. "I'm gonna be strong, just like a superhero. Remember when we talked about being superheroes at Sunday school?"

"I sure do," Fernando answered.

"My granny says 'Greater is He that's in me than he that's in the whole wide world.' She told me that I may have dye beads, but dye beads isn't gonna have me. I like my granny. She smells like cookies," Maggie giggled, revealing a gorgeous set of dimples.

Her innocent joy, even in this hard time, touched the two adults deeply.

"Mommy even says that someday they might find a cure for dye beads," Maggie finished.

Mrs. Walker smiled and kissed her daughter's forehead. "That's right. It's possible, baby."

Fernando remembered Janet's words from Matthew 19:26 and spoke them aloud. "With God, all things are possible."

It was hard to concentrate the rest of the workday. It didn't help that everyone and their mother was rushing to the hardware store to get their last minute icicle lights and giant Santa-in-a-snow-globe lawn ornaments.

As soon as his shift was over, Fernando headed straight home. There was no time to mope around and feel sorry for himself. He had a promise to keep.

Before he'd left the hospital, Maggie had told him, "I miss your stories. I wish you could write a story about a kid with dye beads so other kids like me would know that it's okay not to be scared. You know why?"

"No, tell me why," Fernando answered, blinking and trying to swallow the lump in his throat.

" 'Cause God loves kids."

Mrs. Walker smiled with teary eyes and Fernando nodded as he responded. "He sure does, Maggie. He sure does."

Now he was a man on a mission. He'd barely taken off his jacket when he plopped down in front of the computer. He pulled up everything he could find on juvenile diabetes symptoms, treatments, and parental support groups. He took a moment to pray for wisdom, and then he opened up a new word processing document and began to type.

It was a good thing he had Friday off because he didn't *stop* typing until 4:30 Friday morning. He somehow found his way to the bed; slept for six hours; got up; showered; wolfed down something he wouldn't remember eating later; then pulled out his old sketchpad and began to draw.

## ❧ 6 ❧

*December 11*

"Alright Tim, it's your turn." Fernando was having each child in the Sunday school class sign Maggie's card. She'd had to return to the hospital where the staff was having a difficult time getting her blood sugar regulated, so she would be there for a while longer.

He'd found the huge card at a party supply store. It was nearly as big as the kids were, and they thought it was the coolest thing they'd ever seen. They'd pranced around with excitement, waiting for their turns, until every child had signed it.

Janet stepped into the room as the last student left and laughed. "That's a great idea!"

"Thank you. Are you okay? You look frustrated."

"I'm good. Jeff and I broke up. We had a long talk a couple of days ago and he really isn't ready to settle down."

"Wow, I'm really sorry, Janet. I know you were pretty crazy about him."

"That's the funny part. I actually *wasn't* that crazy about him. I've realized that I was crazy about the idea of being with someone, and about the hope that I could be that someone's wife more than I was crazy about *Jeff*. I need to make sure I'm happy with where I am now before God's gonna bless me with the man I'm supposed to marry and raise a family with."

"So you're okay?"

"Yeah, I'm fine. Really. Thanks for all those times you let me vent."

"Don't even worry about it. I want to thank you for encouraging me to write my stories down too. Maggie inspired me to do this." He reached into his duffel bag, pulled out a book, and handed it to her proudly.

She stared blankly at it until realization dawned on her. Then her face lit up so much that his breath caught unexpectedly. "Oh my goodness, you did it! This is so awesome! But how did you get it published so quickly?"

"You'd be amazed at how many sites are out there that print your stuff like the professionals do and ship it to you."

She couldn't take her eyes off the book. "This is gonna be such an incredible surprise for Maggie. Dude, you are gonna make such a phenomenal dad one day."

He expected to feel that familiar dull ache that always came at the mention of the family he'd hoped to have by now, but it didn't come. It might again in the future, but right now he felt too good about what he'd achieved to worry about what he didn't have.

"Where can I buy one?"

He smiled at her. "This one's yours. I even signed it for you."

The pleasure he'd felt seeing her reaction to the book was incredible. He could hardly wait to show it to Maggie. He arrived at the hospital shortly after church and practically ran all the way to her room.

The Walkers were sitting up with their daughter when he stepped in.

"Good to see you, Fernando." Mr. Walker stood and shook his hand as Mrs. Walker and Maggie both waved at him.

"Hello everyone. Mr. and Mrs. Walker, I'd like to give Maggie a gift if you don't mind."

"That's so sweet of you, but you didn't have to bring a gift."

"It was no trouble at all, Mrs. Walker. I wanted to. See, I promised Maggie I'd write a story about her." He pulled the book out from behind his back with a dramatic flourish. "And here it is!"

Maggie squealed excitedly and clapped her hands.

He took it to her and she pored over every single page, making comments about all the pictures.

Mr. Walker read the title aloud. "I Have Juvenile Diabetes, But It Doesn't Have Me." He immediately recognized his mother's adage and smiled.

"Will you read it to me, Mr. Rodriguez? Mommy, Daddy, will you listen to my story?"

Fernando told her he would read it, and her parents promised her that they would listen to every word.

He sat and read the story of a little girl who found out she had diabetes. He read about the disease and how the doctors helped the little girl treat it, in words Maggie could easily understand. At the end of the story the brave little girl learned to live a happy, healthy life, even though she still had diabetes, because she was made strong by the love of God and her family and friends.

"Yay!" Maggie bounced up and down in her bed and applauded.

Later, when she'd nodded off to sleep, Fernando presented a second book to her parents. "That way, she can keep her copy here, and you can take this one home."

"We don't know what to say, Fernando. Thank you so much. What an incredible gift!" Mrs. Walker gushed.

Mr. Walker pumped Fernando's hand vigorously. "This is one of the most amazing things anyone has ever done for us. God bless you."

Fernando had only bought five copies of the book from the print-on-demand website. He'd given one to Janet, one to Maggie, one to her parents, one to *his* parents (who had gushed as proudly as if he'd been signed to a major publishing company), and he'd kept one for himself.

That night, as he lay in bed thinking on the events of the day, his eyes fell on his copy sitting on his nightstand. He'd never thought he could do such a thing. He'd even scoffed at the idea when Janet mentioned it to him. Yet here the book sat. A book he wrote and illustrated; a book that had blessed a family in need of some joy. He mentally cataloged the highlights of his life and came to the conclusion that nothing he'd done with his own hands had ever made him feel quite so happy or fulfilled.

"Lord, it's a long shot – one I didn't even believe in not too long ago, but if You open a door for me to write books all the time, I promise I'll walk through it. And I'll use it to bless kids and their families."

He finished his prayer and a few short minutes later he drifted off into peaceful sleep.

## ❧ 7 ❧

*December 14*

The Rodriguez cousins, aunts, and uncles lavished their celebrated author with so much praise at Wednesday family night that he finally begged them to stop. "My head's gonna be too big for me to get through the front door. Besides, I keep telling you – it's not a real published book. It's just something I did and had printed."

"It doesn't matter!" his cousin, Marisol had exclaimed. "With this much talent, it's only a matter of time before a publishing deal comes through for you. We won't stop praying until we see it happen!"

Their loving support touched him and reminded him that he wasn't really as alone as he sometimes felt.

That Saturday he visited Maggie and got a wonderful surprise.

Hi, Mr. Rodriguez. I'm going home today!" Her excited proclamation and the huge smile on her face lit up the whole room.

"You are? Oh, Maggie, that's so cool!" He hugged her and congratulated the Walkers.

"We're so happy she's coming home. It's been hard walking past her room and seeing her empty bed." Mrs. Walker's voice was thick with emotion and her eyes were full of joyful tears.

"Oh, yeah! There are some people who want to meet you. I'll be right back," Mr. Walker called over his shoulder as he left the room.

Maggie showed Fernando the drawings she'd made to pass the time as her treatments had brought her insulin levels under control.

He oohed and aahed at all the appropriate junctures as she explained what each picture was.

"And this one is me reading my dye beads story to some of the other kids when I got to go to the playroom. A lot of kids wish they could get a story about why they're sick too."

"They sure do, Maggie."

Fernando looked up at the sound of the new voice and saw a doctor and another man standing in the doorway with Mr. Walker, who introduced them as Dr. Alvin Patterson and Mr. Barry Young.

After handshakes and pleasantries, Dr. Patterson, in typical doctor fashion, got straight to the point.

"Maggie's absolutely right. You're something of a celebrity with many of the children on this floor. We've been getting a lot of requests for books about their various conditions."

Mr. Young spoke up. "The kids with juvenile diabetes even like to pretend the book is about them. I know my son does. The way you explain the process is so easy for kids to understand. That takes some of the fear out of what they're going through."

Dr. Patterson's next words shocked Fernando speechless. "I'd like to suggest that you consider doing more books on some of the other illnesses the children face in our pediatric ward. I think the books could be great teaching tools, and I'd be proud to buy them and keep them stocked in our playroom and in the waiting areas on other floors."

"We think it's a fantastic idea," Mrs. Walker chimed in as Mr. Walker nodded his head in agreement.

Fernando ran his hand over his face in amazement. "I'm really honored, but I wouldn't know the first thing about how to write about other diseases. It took me quite a while just to do the research for this one."

"What if I consulted you? I could give you some basic summaries, enough for you to get the general idea about symptoms and treatment and so on," Dr. Patterson offered.

"Please, Mr. Rodriguez? You could help so many kids, just like you helped me," Maggie pleaded.

He felt a sudden tightening in his throat. "Ah, little one," he sighed, holding his hand over his heart. "How could I say 'no' to such a request?"

"Yay!" She bounced and clapped in her bed until Fernando felt like he could walk on the moon.

He finally came back to Earth and began to work things out in his head. "I need to check the website I get the books printed through to see how many I can order at once."

Mr. Young stopped him. "No need for that. I think I can go one better. Have you ever heard of Young at Heart Publishing?"

"Sure, I have. They publish inspirational books for all ages. I remember seeing them featured on the news because they're local and they work hard to promote local authors."

"That's right. I'm glad to know we have that reputation. My dad started that publishing house fifteen years ago, and you're looking at the editor."

## ❧ 8 ❧

*December 17*

After restocking the last bag of artificial snow that Robby Franklin had cleaned out earlier that evening, Fernando began closing down the hardware store.

He shook his head in wonder at his customer's reformed humbug transformation. The man had come in several times with his wife and neither one of them ever looked like they wanted to be there (or anywhere for that matter) together. She wanted the best stuff and he wanted the cheapest, and that was how the argument always began. They fought so much that Fernando hated to see them walk in the door.

Then today, without warning, Mr. Franklin had waltzed in and bought a cartload of their most expensive artificial snow so that he could give his wife a snow-covered lawn.

Fernando quit trying to figure it out. "Ah well. Christmas miracles do happen," he mused.

He was certainly proof of that. As the newest author for Young at Heart Publishing, he'd received a very nice advance on his "It Doesn't Have Me" series of kids' books. His advance was so nice that he figured he'd stay on at the store until after the holiday rush when the owner would have time to find a replacement for him, and then he'd devote his time to his new career.

His mother had told him God had a purpose for his life. Janet had believed in him even when he hadn't believed in himself. Now he was able to devote himself to his God-given passion for helping kids, because he finally stopped being scared and started using the gifts the Lord had given him.

As he drove home thinking of everything that had happened, he prayed aloud. "Dios usted ha sido muy bueno. Gracias. God, You have been very good to me. Thank you."

## ❧ 9 ❧

*Christmas Eve*

"I love it, Mrs. Winslow. Thank you!"

"I'm glad you like it. It's my newest hobby since I can't knit anymore."

Fernando had stopped by Ella Winslow's house to wish her a Merry Christmas, and she had presented him with a gift basket she'd made. It contained a tape measure, a pocket tool kit, and a beautiful pen for the up-and-coming author.

She looked happier than he'd seen her in a long time, and she even had relatives visiting with her.

He thanked God for answering her prayers as well as his.

They chatted for a few more minutes until the grandfather clock in the hallway chimed six times.

"Well, I'd better go. I have a date!"

Mrs. Winslow's whole face broke into a smile, as if her mouth alone couldn't fully do the job.

"Really! Who is the blessed lady?"

"Someone I've spent time with every week, but never really noticed how wonderful she is."

Mrs. Winslow chuckled. "Isn't that the way? Sometimes our greatest treasures are hiding right under our noses. You have a good time with your young lady. And Merry Christmas."

Fernando planted a reverent kiss on his friend's head. "Feliz Navidad!"

A few minutes later he entered the pediatric ward of the hospital.

"Mr. Rodriguez!" a roomful of children screamed and rushed toward him to hug him.

"Hola, everybody! Are you ready for story time?"

"Yeah!" they shouted in unison.

Like the kids in his Sunday school class, the children sat enraptured as he read, not from one of his own books, but from the second book of Luke. Parents and staff alike watched the tiny patients sit cross-legged or on couches or in wheelchairs as Fernando told the story of Jesus' birth.

When he was done, he taught the group to sing *Feliz Navidad*. Then he gave each of the little ones a hug and a kiss.

As they happily returned his affection, his eyes filled with tears. "Lord, I hope that one day you will bless me with my own, but even if that day never comes, I thank You that I have a whole room full of kids."

"I keep telling you – you are gonna make the most awesome dad one of these days."

Fernando looked up and smiled. "Hey Janet. You look great."

She rolled her eyes and laughed. "Please. I'm still wearing my scrubs."

"What does that have to do with anything? You still look great," he replied with a wink.

She smiled and ducked her head before he could see how much his compliment pleased her. "I just finished my shift. Give me ten minutes to change and we can go to dinner."

True to her word, she came back exactly ten minutes later. She was wearing a pretty blue sweater dress and calf-high heeled boots. She'd taken down her eternal ponytail and her dark brown hair fell past her shoulders. She'd even applied a touch of lipstick and blush.

Fernando had only seen her working with the kids in Sunday school and here at the hospital when she was on duty. He'd never seen her like this before, and he was blown away. "You looked great before. Now you look *incredible*."

She started to reply when one of the kids interrupted. "Janet, are you and Fernando going on a date?"

"Yup, we sure are," she answered. Then she crossed her eyes and stuck out her tongue.

The kids thought the date and the face she made were hilarious and the room filled with their giggles and snorts. Soon they started to sing.

"Janet and Fernando sittin' in a tree…"

"Hey!" Janet tried to scold them, but her smile ruined the effect. "Nobody's gonna be kissing anybody in some old tree, so you just knock that off."

That made them laugh even harder, and finally she and Fernando gave up and joined in the merriment.

*Christmas Day*

Christmas service at Blessed Savior Church was a festive event. The congregation had many young families, so there was never a shortage of children in the annual Christmas play.

Fernando and Janet sat together during worship, slipping one another shy smiles every so often.

The congregation was just small enough to notice when a lone family entered the sanctuary a little late. Service literally stopped as everyone gazed at the family, not in censure, but with joy.

Pastor Marcus spoke into the microphone. "If any among us wonder if God still works miracles, we have only to look at the back of the church to see one. Welcome back, Maggie. We prayed long and hard for the Lord to bring you back to us, and He did. Praise God!"

Maggie Walker and her parents smiled and waved as the church broke into spontaneous cheers and shouts of praise and thanksgiving.

As she sat perched on her father's hip, Maggie's eyes scanned the crowd until she spotted Fernando, then she began waving wildly. He winked at her and gave a subtle wave back. He didn't want to take one moment of attention away from the amazing little girl who helped give him the gift he'd needed most – knowing God's purpose for his life.

# Ella's Gift

Shout for joy, O heavens! And rejoice, O earth!
Break forth into joyful shouting, O mountains!
For the LORD has comforted His people
and will have compassion on His afflicted.
- Isaiah 49:13

*November 25*

Ella Winslow sat in the recliner next to the big picture window in her living room. An afghan she'd knitted when her fingers had been nimbler warmed her tired bones. Arthritis had claimed her fingers and stolen her hobby, just as old age and illness had claimed her husband, Edgar, just two years before.

Thanksgiving had just passed, and she was ashamed to admit that for most of the day it had been hard to give thanks. She'd sat in that very chair and cried for what seemed like hours because she was alone on Thanksgiving Day.

Her husband was gone, and her daughter was never around long enough to count.

Angela had been their miracle child – the one the doctor said they wouldn't be able to have. Ella never understood how such a blessing could have turned into such a nightmare.

"Enough of that." She shook her head as if that would shake off the gloomy sentiment. She brought her mind back to the present and reminded herself that things had gotten much better later on Thanksgiving Day. A little after one in the afternoon, her neighbor, Fernando Rodriguez, had stopped by to sit with her for a while. No more than an hour after he left, her good friend from church, Helen Carter, came to sit with her.

They'd chatted over coffee for hours, both women desperately needing the companionship.

"Has Angela come to visit you today, Ella?"

"Ha! She came to visit *you* if she visited me. I don't even know what state she's living in these days."

"What is the matter with that girl? She couldn't even call her mother on Thanksgiving Day?"

"I gave up trying to understand Angela a long time ago, Helen. She had a solid upbringing in a home with parents who loved her, but she was always a wild child. She gave Eddie and me no end of problems."

"I remember how that child used to carry on. If there was devilment to be had, she found it."

"That's sure the truth. Angela didn't just get into trouble. She wallowed in it. You should have seen her the minute she turned eighteen. She shot out of this house so fast she almost tore the door off its hinges."

"The two of you did the best you could, Ella. Nobody blamed either of you for how her life turned out."

Ella had shaken her head sadly. By age twenty-two her daughter had become a veteran on the club scene; by twenty-four she'd gotten into drugs, alcohol, and God knew what else; and at twenty-seven, she had given birth to Ella's granddaughter, Cathy. At least that event had allowed the Winslows to see their daughter a little more often. If she couldn't find a babysitter when she wanted to go do whatever it was she did, Ella and Eddie got a chance to spend time with their granddaughter.

She was a sweet little girl with skin the color of a Hershey's kiss, lopsided braids, and clothes that never seemed to fit quite right. The doting grandparents lavished all the love on Cathy that Angela, for whatever reason, had always rejected.

Helen seemed to read her thoughts. "I guess that means you haven't heard from Cathy either."

"Since that baby turned twelve and Angela moved out of town, I can count the number of times I've seen her on one hand."

"Oh, Ella! I'm so sorry. I know how much you and Eddie loved that girl. It's probably not her fault. It's that mama of hers."

"I know it is. Cathy even wrote to us for a while after they moved, but then that stopped. I don't blame the baby, although I can't rightly call her a baby anymore. If my math is right, she's about twenty-two now. I pray she's alright, and that her life has turned out better than her mother's."

"Amen to that," Helen had wholeheartedly agreed. "I'd better go. It's getting a mite dark and I can't drive as well at night."

"Helen, you just don't know how much your visit means to me." Ella was embarrassed by the moisture she felt building in her eyes.

Her friend touched her arm gently. "I understand. Young folks don't always realize how lonely we can get, especially when our husbands have passed. That's why we've got to look out for each other."

Just those two visits on Thanksgiving Day, that human contact, had made all the difference in Ella's outlook. Now, as she remembered how her mood had brightened after that, she came to a determined realization.

"I can't go on like this too much longer. If I don't start living again, I'm surely going to die."

She decided then and there that she wouldn't waste away from inactivity and loneliness. She would find something to engage her mind and spirit and get her back among people. She would begin to truly live again before emptiness and hopelessness claimed her very life.

The only problem was that she didn't know how. So Ella Winslow did what she always did when she was at a loss for answers: she prayed.

"Father God, I need to feel happiness again. Eddie's with You, and only You know where Angela and her family are. Until You decide to call me home, please bring some joy back into my life."

## ❧ 2 ❦

*November 27*

"Good morning, Mother Winslow."

"Hello, Mother. You're looking mighty fine in that royal blue suit today!"

As she stepped into Mount Sinai Church and made her way to her favorite seat, Ella nodded politely to each person and gave her trademark reply: "Hello, child. God bless you."

Helen scooted over to make room for her on the pew. "I like that blue on you. Cool colors always did look nice on your fair skin."

"Thank you. Oh, Helen! Where ever did you find that hat? It's beautiful!" Ella exclaimed.

The two women talked amiably until Deacon Taylor stepped up to the podium to begin devotion.

"Let us be in prayer for our pastor's sister, Mother Gentry. She had a heart attack this past week. Thank the Lord she made it through, but she still needs our prayers."

Gasps of shock were heard around the sanctuary at the deacon's announcement. Ella and Helen clasped hands. Beatrice Gentry was one of their dearest friends. They decided to visit her at the hospital immediately after service.

Deacon Taylor's rich tenor voice rang out as he began a spiritual.

The organist skimmed the keys to find the right note, then immediately picked up the song. The congregation joined in and the whole room became a choir as they sang together in harmony.

The deacon began to pray in song. He cried out to God on behalf of the unsaved, the sick and shut-in, and the bereaved. He prayed protection on the youth and comfort for the afflicted.

One by one, voices began to join in the prayer song.

"Yes, Lord!"

"We're waiting on You, Father!"

"Come on, Jesus!"

The toddlers and younger kids in the church often fell asleep right about now, but anyone who was going through something knew the power of prayer, and this was one of their most beloved times.

Women stood with their eyes closed and rocked from side to side. Men knelt at the pews and covered their faces in their hands. The older members who could neither kneel nor stand for long periods of time sat in their seats with their hands uplifted.

If anyone ever wondered what "Sweet Hour of Prayer" looked like in practice, all they had to do was visit Mount Sinai Church.

## ❧ 3 ❧

"Beatrice, we didn't have any idea you were sick. Otherwise you know we would have been here."

Ella smoothed her friend's silver hair and took a seat next to her.

Mother Gentry smiled and nodded. "I know. I sure do thank you for coming now. It's good to see you."

"Mm hm. We missed seeing what kind of hat you would wear today."

Beatrice chuckled at Helen's comment. Her Sunday hats were a gravitational wonder as they sat perched perfectly atop a head half their mammoth size.

She tapped her mouth with her finger thoughtfully. "I remember – I was going to wear the purple one."

"Ooh, the one with the plumes on it?" Ella touched her friend's arm. "I've always admired that hat."

The women talked of church clothes and younger days. Helen, with her quick wit, had them all in stitches as she reenacted some of the scenes from the service, and Ella read aloud from the Psalms.

"Goodness! We've been here two hours!" Helen finally exclaimed. "We'd better go and let you rest."

"Alright, but your visit did me just as much good as sleep will do." She quoted Proverbs 17:22. 'A joyful heart is good medicine, but a broken spirit dries up the bones.' The two of you have certainly brought some laughter to these old bones. God bless the both of you."

The praise touched both women immensely. They joined hands with her and prayed for her speedy recovery, gave her parting hugs, and then walked to the parking lot together.

Helen sighed. "I haven't felt that useful in a long time, Ella."

"I know what you mean. It felt good to do something to help somebody, and know that they appreciate it." Ella fell silent for a long moment.

"I know that look, Ella Winslow. You're hatching something up. If it involves the slightest bit of mischief I demand to be included."

Ella giggled and squeezed her friend's hand. "There's no way I'd try doing it without you. Let's go have some coffee and start plotting."

## ❧ **4** ❧

*November 30*

"Do you want to go see Beatrice with me?"

Ella didn't hesitate as she spoke into the telephone. "Helen, I've been all dressed up with nowhere to go since 7 'o clock this morning. Come on through and get me."

A few minutes later, she slid into her friend's car carrying a package.

Helen peered at the object she had in her hands. "What do you have there? And don't tell me to quit being nosey and watch the road because I haven't even started driving yet."

Ella chuckled as she held up her treasure for inspection. "I wanted to knit something for Bea, but you know Uncle Arthur messed with my hands so much that I can't do it anymore. I decided to make her a gift basket instead. The ones in the gift store were so expensive, and besides, you know how persnickety Bea is. Those store-bought baskets don't have anything in them she would like anyway."

"Oh, but yours does! She'll love everything in it. What a wonderful idea!" Helen gushed.

The pretty little basket was covered in shiny cellophane. It was purple of course – Beatrice's favorite color. Inside was a small pocket Bible, a bag of Butterscotch (also her favorite), and a rack of extra large hat pins.

At the sight of the pins, Helen leaned back and laughed until her eyes watered. "Ella, you are too much!"

"Well, how else can she keep those cake plate sized hats on her head? You know she must use at least twenty pins a Sunday."

Helen laughed even harder then, and soon Ella was guffawing right along with her.

When they shared the story with Beatrice, she laughed harder than either of them.

"I tell you, you two are a tonic. A lot of sick and hurting people would be mighty blessed if they got wonderful visits like this."

"Well, since you mentioned it, we are going to talk to pastor about an idea I had," Ella leaned in and whispered conspiringly.

"Oh! Are you going to start a board?"

"Heavens no! We've already got an elder's board, a mother's board, a deacon's board, and an usher's board. I don't want to start another board. I'm 'board' to death. I just want to do something to help people who are lonely and hurting."

"We know what that feels like, don't we, Bea?" Helen asked sadly.

"We sure do. It's hard when you're dealing with death or illness. When you're a widow with grown kids that are out of the house, and maybe even out of state, you feel like you're all alone sometimes. Tell me more about this idea. I think I like it already. If my brother gives you a lick of trouble when you talk to him about it, you just let me know."

## ❧ 5 ❧

*December 4*

Like many of the seniors at Mount Sinai, Ella didn't attend mid-week Bible study because she didn't trust herself driving at night. For that reason, she and Helen had waited all week, somewhat impatiently, to share their suggestion with Pastor Jones.

The wait was worth it. They explained their plan to him in the twenty minutes between Sunday school and service. He absolutely loved the idea, and was so excited about it that he told them he would mention it to the congregation during announcements.

After the lively service, Sister Clark took her place at the podium and read the highlights from the church bulletin. As she finished, she added "We have one more announcement from our pastor."

Pastor Jones stood and spoke into the pulpit microphone. "Thank you, Sister Clark. I'm very excited to tell you that Mother Winslow and Mother Carter came to me this morning with a wonderful idea. Many of our older members want to feel useful in the church. They have gifts and abilities just like the younger folks. These two ladies are going to give you a new opportunity to serve at Mount Sinai.

Mothers, would you wave your hands so everybody can see you?"

Ella and Helen smiled and waved, tickled pink by all the unexpected attention they were getting.

"They have started a ministry, with my blessing, called Comforting Grace. They will manage a team of volunteers, mostly retired folks, although young people can be a part as well. Those on the team will visit members in the hospital or if they're sick at home. They also plan to start visiting some of our members who are now permanently homebound or in nursing homes. If you're interested in joining this ministry, see Mother Winslow or Mother Carter after service."

Any concerns the ladies might have had about lack of interest in their mission were quickly squashed. Many of the older members (and some younger ones as well), both women and men, signed up to be a part of the new ministry. By the time Mount Sinai's parking lot had cleared out for the day, Comforting Grace was already a dozen volunteers strong.

Two days later, gift baskets, ribbon, cellophane, and various other supplies covered the dining room table after Ella's trip to the arts and crafts store.

Helen had told the other members of Comforting Grace about the wonderful basket her friend had made Beatrice. They all thought the personalized gifts were a lovely idea to give some of the people they would be visiting.

Pastor Jones had even given Ella a modest budget so she wouldn't have to pay for the supplies out of her own fixed income. She'd gone earlier in the day to get everything she needed for her first batch of baskets.

She'd also met a new friend, a nice young woman named Tammy Franklin. She was a painter and had given Ella her business card.

"I've got to remember to call her. Even though she was very friendly, she seemed so sad."

She organized her new supplies and neatly put them away, humming "What a Friend We Have in Jesus" all the while. Next she put on a fresh pot of coffee and arranged some tea cakes she'd baked on a serving platter. Comforting Grace was having its first official meeting at her house in less than an hour.

"To think," she said with a smile, "Two weeks ago I thought I would waste away from loneliness. Now I'm entertaining guests and helping other people. Lord, You sure do know how to answer prayer."

## ❧ 6 ❧

*December 15*

It was nearly 9 'o clock and Ella was just getting ready to go to bed.

The past week had been very fulfilling. She'd visited Beatrice, who was back at home, as well as two of her other friends who now lived in nursing homes.

She had spent the afternoon with them talking about their health, their younger days, and the happenings at Mount Sinai. She even brought them gift baskets, which they loved.

"Hardly anybody comes to visit anymore," Edith had said. "I'm so glad you came."

"You're the first visitor I've had in three weeks. Please come back soon," James had implored.

Yes, the week had been fulfilling, but it had been very busy as well, and she was tired.

Just as she turned the doorknob to her bedroom, the doorbell rang.

"Hmph! I like that. Ringing an old woman's doorbell this time of night." She made her way to the front door and peered through the curtain. A young woman was standing there with two small children.

Ella opened the door and the woman looked at her with a combination of relief and uncertainty. She shifted a toddler in her arms and clutched the hand of the other child, who couldn't have been more than six.

Instantly, a wave of familiarity hit Ella. The set of the woman's eyes and the chocolate color of her skin reminded her of …

"Cathy?"

The woman immediately burst into tears.

"Come on in, child. Let's get these babies out of the cool night air." Ella herded the small family into the house.

Once they were in the living room Cathy stood the toddler on his feet, and before Ella knew what happened she found herself enveloped in her granddaughter's arms.

"Gramma! It's been so long, and I wasn't sure if I remembered how to get to your house. I'm so glad I found you."

"Goodness, you're shaking. There, there. It's alright." She held Cathy and stroked her back gently until she felt some of the tension subside.

"Mama!" the toddler yelled worriedly, tugging on her pant leg.

Cathy looked down and rubbed his head. "Mama's okay, Dex. Meet your great-gramma. Reggie, say 'hi' to great-gramma."

The older child, who had been sitting on the couch quietly staring at everyone, spoke softly. "Hi."

"Lord, have mercy. These are your babies?"

"Yes, ma'am."

"Dexter and Reggie," Ella repeated, and the kids perked up at the sound of their names.

"Well, Dexter, you're as cute as a button." She tapped his little nose, causing him to giggle and bury his face shyly in his mother's pant leg.

"And Reggie, you're quite the handsome young man. May I have a hug?"

He shook his head up and down, then reached up and gave her a hug.

Unexpectedly, tears sprang up in her eyes. "Goodness, gracious. I'm sorry I'm so emotional. Cathy, you don't know how often I've thought about you and prayed for you over the years. Now to see you and your children …it's just so amazing! How is…" She paused, almost too afraid to finish asking the question.

Cathy understood. "How is Mama?" She shrugged sadly. "Same as always. I'm so sorry I lost touch with you, Gramma. We moved around so much, and things got so bad that for a while, I got angry with you and Grandpa. I felt like you guys should have taken me from her so I could have a normal life with you. Eventually, I realized it wasn't your fault any more than it was mine. But then I couldn't find your address anymore. I asked Mama if we could visit you, but she always made some excuse."

Ella sat forlornly on the couch and put her head in her hands. "I don't understand what happened with her. We tried everything we could, but she just couldn't get her life together. Maybe we were too strict. I just don't know."

Cathy touched her grandmother's leg. "It wasn't your fault. I don't even think it was hers. Some people are just mean and impossible to understand all their lives. Relatives say that's just how they are, but I think a lot of times it's mental illness. Who knows how her life would have turned out if she'd gotten some treatment and some medication? All our lives might have turned out differently."

Ella thought long and hard. "You may be right. In my time, nobody talked about mental problems. If you went to a psychiatrist or something, people said you were crazy. I wish I knew then what I know now."

She looked at the face of the granddaughter she hadn't seen in years, and the great-grandchildren she'd never seen, and despite her pain, her mood began to lighten.

"At least Angela is alive. As long as we're breathing, we have a chance to get it right. Now come sit down by me and tell me what brought this blessing to my front door."

*December 17*

"So they're staying with you?" Helen asked after Ella explained the events of the past couple of days.

Shifting the phone to her other ear, Ella continued working on her latest gift basket. "They sure are. Imagine: children in my house again!"

"I *can* imagine. That's why I'm wondering if you're going to get tired of all that noise after a while."

"I probably will," Ella replied, chuckling. "But I promised Cathy that they could stay here until she finds a place. She finally got tired of her mama's ways. She's grown now, so when Angela moved again, chasing after some man, she decided she'd had enough. She came looking for the only stable family she'd ever known, and I'm not about to turn her away. This house is big enough for all of us, and Lord knows it's been lonely around here for far too long."

"How did she take the news that Eddie passed?"

"Oh, Helen! You should have seen her. She asked where he was, and when I told her he died two years ago, she just sat there quiet as a church mouse. 'If I would have known, I would have come, Gramma.

I'm so sorry.' She just kept saying that and crying. That child cried so hard that she set *me* to crying."

"Poor thing. Is she there now?"

"Naw, she's looking for a job and trying to enroll in evening classes too. I told her school won't do nothin' but help. She seems like she's trying to get her life together."

"I hope things work out for all of you. Ooh, I need to go. My water pill just started working."

Ella stifled a giggle and said goodbye to her friend. She put the finishing touches on Tammy's gift basket and sat back to inspect it. She'd finally remembered to call the woman earlier that day, and was glad she had.

Tammy's troubled marriage had taken a turn for the better, and she'd asked Ella for a 'just because' gift to give her husband, Robby.

"I think this will do just fine." She covered the basket in cellophane and attached a red bow. Just then she felt a gentle tug on her skirt and looked down to find a little person eyeing the nearly empty bag of walnut halves she'd been using for the gift basket.

"Well, hello Dexter. Would you like some of these walnuts?"

"Some?" he repeated with outstretched hands.

She used the tip of the nutcracker to break a piece into smaller bites.

The boy gingerly accepted the tiny chunk and chewed it with great concentration before reaching up for another piece.

Ella laughed until she had to wipe her eyes. "Bless my soul. A man who likes walnuts is alright with me."

Reggie ran into the room holding the handset. "Great-gramma. The telephone is for you."

"Thank you, baby. Do you want some walnuts?"

The older boy looked suspiciously at the nuts before shaking his head. "No, ma'am, but can I have some of your peppermints?"

"You sure can."

He was out of the room in a flash.

"Just get two, Reggie. Don't spoil your dinner," she called out after him.

Dexter tugged on her skirt again.

"That's alright. It just means more for us, doesn't it?" she cooed as she handed him another chunk, then answered the phone.

"Ella, it's Beatrice. I've got some sad news. Do you remember visiting James Burns last week? Well, he passed away last night."

## ❧ 8 ❦

*Christmas Eve*

"It must have been really hard for the family burying Mr. Burns right before Christmas."

Ella sighed and shook her head. "There's never a good time to lose a loved one, but holidays are extra hard. James loved the Lord though, Cathy, so we know we'll see him again."

Ella had begun to share the Gospel with her granddaughter in small ways. She didn't force it on her, but she planted the seed.

"Will that make it hard for you and that group from your church to keep visiting people? I don't know if I'd want to do that for a while after something like this happened."

"No, child. If anything, it makes me more determined to keep doing it. Do you know what one of the nurses told me? She said that someone from our church group either came to visit him or called him twice a week, and that was more than his own family did. He talked a lot about how much he looked forward to our company. That was a great comfort to him in his final days."

"You're pretty cool, Gramma." Cathy rose and planted a kiss on Ella's surprised forehead.

"Well, thank you, baby." She chuckled and shook her head. "I don't think anybody's ever told me that before."

"Great-gramma, somebody's coming to your door." Reggie called. He'd been playing in the living room and saw the visitor approaching.

"Door!" Dexter echoed.

"I'll get it, Gramma," Cathy offered. She reached the door and pulled it open just as the bell rang.

A man stood there with a surprised look on his face. "Hello. I'm here to see Mrs. Winslow. My name is Fernando Rodriguez."

"Oh, Gramma told me about you. You're the author, right? That's tight! I'm Cathy. It's nice to meet you."

She let Fernando in and shook his hand just as Ella walked up.

"Merry Christmas, Fernando."

He gave her a hug. "Feliz Navidad, Mrs. Winslow. I just came to visit for a little while on Christmas Eve."

"How nice! Come on in and have a seat. You've already met my granddaughter. Let me introduce you to my great-grandchildren, Reggie and Dexter."

Dexter had retreated behind Cathy's leg. He peeked around it and waved shyly.

Fernando leaned down, winked at him and waved back, which caused the toddler to giggle.

Reggie looked up curiously at the man. "What did you say before? It didn't make sense."

Fernando laughed. "I said 'Feliz Navidad.' It's Spanish and it means 'Merry Christmas.' "

"Oh!" Reggie seemed to think that was pretty awesome and began trying to say the phrase under his breath.

"I can teach you how to say it," Fernando offered. He sat on the floor next to the boy and taught him how to sound the words out.

A couple of minutes later, Reggie jumped up and proudly called out "Feliz Navidad!"

The adults clapped and cheered for him, which caused Dexter to shriek and clap excitedly too.

Ella presented her friend with a gift basket she'd made to thank him for all the times he stopped by to help her. She mused that she probably loved giving him the gift as much as he loved receiving it.

They sat laughing and talking for a few minutes more until he announced that he had a date. Ella was elated. She had often prayed for him to find a nice woman who would appreciate his gentle spirit.

After he left, she spent the rest of the evening watching Christmas movies with her family. She couldn't remember enjoying Christmas Eve that much since Eddie went on to glory.

*Christmas Day*

Mount Sinai was all abuzz for Christmas service. The sanctuary was brightly decorated; the angel choir sang Christmas carols in their cute little white robes; the junior Sunday school class recited the second chapter of Luke; and Mother Beatrice Gentry was well enough to return to church.

Everyone knew she was there before they ever saw her. It was the big purple hat that gave her away.

Sister Clark finished reading the announcements and then looked up at the congregation. "We would like to acknowledge our visitors on this blessed Christmas Day. Would any visitors please stand?"

A young family stood and everyone clapped.

Ella couldn't help but burst with pride and she called out, "That's my granddaughter, Cathy, and her children!" She clasped hands happily with Beatrice and Helen.

Sister Clark forgot she was at the microphone. "Cathy? We haven't seen you in years! Those are your babies? You all are just some little cutie pies! Well, look at that! Girl, it's so good to see you and your family!"

When the members heard that, they began to clap in earnest. Many of them remembered Ella and Eddie's struggles with Angela. They even remembered seeing Cathy a few times as a child when she would come to church with her grandparents. They understood the reason for the happiness etched on Ella's face and overflowing in her heart.

She had endured so much pain over the years, but God had brought her through. This Christmas He gave her a gift too wonderful for words. He surrounded her with the comfort of her loved ones, and through her, He spread joy and comfort to many others as well.

### *A note from the author*

First of all, Merry Christmas!

I love this time of year. Mind you, I'm not a cold and snow person at all. I just love the spirit of love, family, and community this season evokes.

Most of all, I'm thankful for the day (in whatever month it actually happened) that Love came down to dwell among us.

I hope *Three Gifts* has evoked some good feelings in you as well. If so, I'd love to hear from you. Drop me a line at www.enorabooks.com or on Facebook at www.facebook.com/EnoraBooks.

Peace and blessings,

Abby Phillips